# GREAT HAIR

TODD PARR

# GREAT HAIR

## TODD PARR

LITTLE, BROWN & COMPANY

LB kids

Some kids have tall hair.

Some kids have small hair.

# Some kids have red hair.

# Some kids have bed hair.

Some kids have hat hair.

Some kids have bat hair.

Some kids have rainbow hair.

Some kids have bow hair.

Some kids have straight hair.

All kids have
great hair!

G  H I J

# LEARNING PAGE

## SIGHT WORDS: some, have

Point to each sight word and read it aloud.

| some | have | some | have |
|------|------|------|------|
| some | some | have | have |
| have | some | have | some |

## BRAIN-BOOSTING QUESTIONS

1. The kids in this book have different kinds of hair. Can you remember them all? Give it a try.
2. What kind of hair do you have? Think of three or more words to describe it.

## EXTRA

Draw and write some brand-new pages for this book. Then read them to a grown-up.

R  Q  P   O  N

K L M

# Welcome to the world of Todd Parr!

## Todd inspires and empowers children around the world with fun, positive messages.

Stories by Todd Parr and Liza Charlesworth
Cover art © 2022 by Todd Parr
Cover design by Lynn El-Roeiy
Cover © 2022 Hachette Book Group, Inc.

Visit us at LBYR.com
toddparr.com
978-0-316-30025-4
Not for Individual Resale

# BE KIND TO ANIMALS

TODD PARR

 • Little, Brown and Company • Hachette Book Group • 1290 Avenue of the Americas, New York, NY 10104 • LB kids is an imprint of Little, Brown and Company. The LB kids name and logo are trademarks of Hachette Book Group, Inc. • The publisher is not responsible for websites (or their content) that are not owned by the publisher. • Distributed in Europe by Little, Brown Book Group UK, Carmelite House, 50 Victoria Embankment, London, EC4Y 0DZ • First Edition: July 2022 • ISBN: 978-0-316-30198-5 • Printed in China • APS • 10 9 8 7 6 5 4 3 2 1

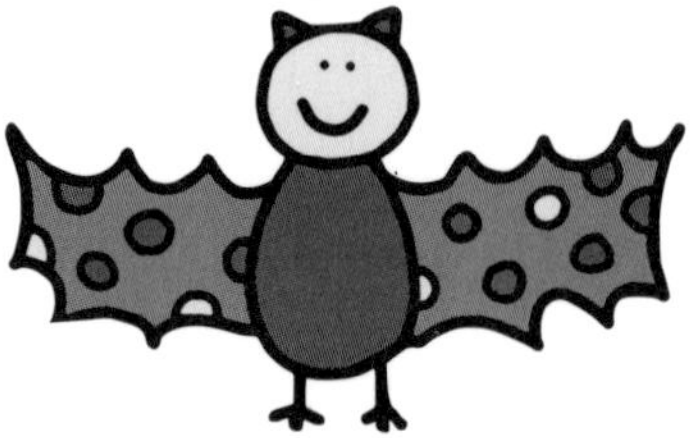

# BE KIND
# TO ANIMALS

HELLO!

## TODD PARR

LITTLE, BROWN & COMPANY
LB kids

# Be kind to cats!

# Be kind to bats!

# Be kind to dogs!

# Be kind to frogs!

# Be kind to elephants!

# Be kind to bears!

Be kind to
all animals!

F  G  H  I  J

# LEARNING PAGE

### SIGHT WORDS: be, to

Point to each sight word and read it aloud.

| be | to | to | be |
|----|----|----|----|
| to | be | to | be |
| to | to | be | be |

 K

 L

## BRAIN-BOOSTING QUESTIONS

1. Why is it important to be kind to animals? Talk about it.
2. What things can people do to help animals? Make a list.

 ★

## EXTRA

Cut out pictures of a favorite animal (from magazines and/or computer printouts) to make a colorful collage. At the top of the paper, write "Be Kind to _____!"

 M

 R  Q  P  O  ♥  ★   N

# Welcome to the world of Todd Parr!

## Todd inspires and empowers children around the world with fun, positive messages.

Stories by Todd Parr and Liza Charlesworth
Cover art © 2022 by Todd Parr
Cover design by Lynn El-Roeiy
Cover © 2022 Hachette Book Group, Inc.

LITTLE, BROWN & COMPANY
LB kids™
NEW YORK  BOSTON

Visit us at LBYR.com
toddparr.com
978-0-316-30198-5
Not for Individual Resale

# PIG AND DOG

TODD PARR

# PIG AND DOG

## TODD PARR

LITTLE, BROWN & COMPANY
LB kids

# Pig and Dog are happy.

# Pig and Dog are hungry.

# Pig and Dog are mad.

# Pig and Dog are proud.

Pig and Dog are silly.

Pig and Dog are surprised.

# Pig and Dog are happy.

F  G  H ♡ I ✦ J

# LEARNING PAGE

### SIGHT WORDS: and, are

Point to each sight word and read it aloud.

| and | and | are | are |
|-----|-----|-----|-----|
| are | and | are | and |
| and | are | are | and |

## BRAIN-BOOSTING QUESTIONS

1. What feelings do Pig and Dog experience in this book? Make a list.
2. What makes you happy? Sad? Surprised? Mad? Talk about it.

## EXTRA

Fire up your imagination to create some brand-new stories starring Pig and Dog.

 R ♥ Q  P  O ♡ N

# Welcome to the world of Todd Parr!

## Todd inspires and empowers children around the world with fun, positive messages.

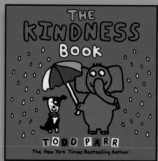

Stories by Todd Parr and Liza Charlesworth
Cover art © 2022 by Todd Parr
Cover design by Lynn El-Roeiy
Cover © 2022 Hachette Book Group, Inc.

LITTLE, BROWN & COMPANY
LB kids™
NEW YORK BOSTON

Visit us at LBYR.com
toddparr.com
978-0-316-30208-1
Not for Individual Resale

# WE CAN SHARE

BOOK

TODD PARR

# WE CAN SHARE

## TODD PARR

LITTLE, BROWN & COMPANY

**LB kids**

We can share a chair.

# We can share a bear.

We can share a book.

# We can share a cone.

# We can share a train.

# We can share a desk.

# We can share a present.

We can share a dog.

We can share a slide.

# We can share a ride!

# LEARNING PAGE

## SIGHT WORDS: we, can, a

Point to each sight word and read it aloud.

| we | can | a | can |
|----|-----|---|-----|
| can | a | we | a |
| a | we | can | we |

## BRAIN-BOOSTING QUESTIONS

1. Can you remember all the things the kids in the story share? Give it a try.
2. Why is it important to share? Talk about it.

## EXTRA

What other things can be shared? Make a long list and hang it on your refrigerator to inspire you every day.

# Welcome to the world of Todd Parr!

## Todd inspires and empowers children around the world with fun, positive messages.

Stories by Todd Parr and Liza Charlesworth
Cover art © 2022 by Todd Parr
Cover design by Lynn El-Roeiy
Cover © 2022 Hachette Book Group, Inc.

LITTLE, BROWN & COMPANY
LB kids™
NEW YORK  BOSTON

Visit us at LBYR.com
toddparr.com
978-0-316-30218-0
Not for Individual Resale

# SEE THE BABY

TODD PARR

• Little, Brown and Company • Hachette Book Group • 1290 Avenue of the Americas, New York, NY 10104 • LB kids is an imprint of Little, Brown and Company. The LB kids name and logo are trademarks of Hachette Book Group, Inc. • The publisher is not responsible for websites (or their content) that are not owned by the publisher. • Distributed in Europe by Little, Brown Book Group UK, Carmelite House, 50 Victoria Embankment, London, EC4Y 0DZ • First Edition: July 2022 • ISBN: 978-0-316-30228-9 • Printed in China • APS • 10  9  8  7  6  5  4  3  2  1

# SEE THE BABY

TODD PARR

LITTLE, BROWN & COMPANY
LB kids

See the baby crawl.

# See the baby cry.

# See the baby read.

# See the baby eat.

# See the baby throw.

# See the baby burp.

# See the baby sleep.

# See the baby peek.

See the baby laugh.

# See the baby hug.

★ **G**  **H** ♥ **I** ★ **J**

# LEARNING PAGE

## SIGHT WORDS: see, the

Point to each sight word and read it aloud.

| the | see | see | the |
|-----|-----|-----|-----|
| see | the | the | see |
| the | see | the | see |

♥

*L*

## BRAIN-BOOSTING QUESTIONS

1. Can you remember all the things the baby in this book does? What else can a baby do? Make a list.
2. Can you think of five or more words to describe a baby? Give it a try.

## EXTRA

Revisit favorite baby photos and videos. How are you the same? How are you different? What have you learned?

 ♥       ♥

# Welcome to the world of Todd Parr!

## Todd inspires and empowers children around the world with fun, positive messages.

Stories by Todd Parr and Liza Charlesworth
Cover art © 2022 by Todd Parr
Cover design by Lynn El-Roeiy
Cover © 2022 Hachette Book Group, Inc.

LB kids

Visit us at LBYR.com
toddparr.com
978-0-316-30228-9
Not for Individual Resale

# SUPER STARS!

# TODD PARR

LITTLE, BROWN & COMPANY

**LB kids**

That bunny is super.
Go, Super Bunny!

That robot is super.
Go, Super Robot!

That skunk is super.
Go, Super Skunk!

That monster is super.
Go, Super Monster!

That bee is super.
Go, Super Bee!

That cookie is super.
Go, Super Cookie!

That snake is super.

# Go, Super Snake!

That ghost is super.
Go, Super Ghost!

That shark is super.
Go, Super Shark!

That star is super.
Go, Super Star!

# LEARNING PAGE

## SIGHT WORDS: that, is, go

Point to each sight word and read it aloud.

| go | is | is | that |
|------|------|------|------|
| is | that | go | go |
| that | go | is | that |

## BRAIN-BOOSTING QUESTIONS

1. Which super star is your very favorite? What other super stars could be in this book? Make a silly list.
2. If you were a super star, what would you do to help the world? Talk about it.

## EXTRA

Make up a story about one of the super stars in this book. What problem does that super star face? How do they save the day?

# Welcome to the world of Todd Parr!

## Todd inspires and empowers children around the world with fun, positive messages.

Stories by Todd Parr and Liza Charlesworth
Cover art © 2022 by Todd Parr
Cover design by Lynn El-Roeiy
Cover © 2022 Hachette Book Group, Inc.

Visit us at LBYR.com
toddparr.com
978-0-316-30238-8
Not for Individual Resale

# I LOVE COLORS!

TODD PARR

# I LOVE COLORS!

# TODD PARR

LITTLE, BROWN & COMPANY

**LB kids**

I love this bird!
It is red.

I love this frog!
It is blue.

I love this dinosaur!

It is yellow.

I love this butterfly!
It is green.

I love this unicorn!
It is orange.

I love this cow!

It is purple.

I love this monster!
It is pink.

I love this rainbow!

I love colors.
I love rainbows.
Yay!

G  H  I  J

# LEARNING PAGE

## SIGHT WORDS: I, this, it, is

Point to each sight word and read it aloud.

| I | it | is | this |
|------|------|------|------|
| this | I | it | is |
| it | is | this | I |

## BRAIN-BOOSTING QUESTIONS

1. Can you remember all the colors mentioned in this book? Can you think of more? Give it a try.
2. What is your favorite color? What things are that color? Talk about it.

## EXTRA

Go on a color hunt in your home. Choose a color and then see if you can find at least five items that are the same color or shade.

R  Q  P  O  N

# Welcome to the world of Todd Parr!

## Todd inspires and empowers children around the world with fun, positive messages.

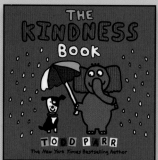

Stories by Todd Parr and Liza Charlesworth
Cover art © 2022 by Todd Parr
Cover design by Lynn El-Roeiy
Cover © 2022 Hachette Book Group, Inc.

LITTLE, BROWN & COMPANY
LB kids™
NEW YORK BOSTON

Visit us at LBYR.com
toddparr.com
978-0-316-30246-3
Not for Individual Resale

# GOOD NIGHT, FARM

TODD PARR

# GOOD NIGHT, FARM

TODD PARR

LITTLE, BROWN & COMPANY
LB kids

# Now the pig will say good night.

# Now the sheep will say good night.

Now the horse will say good night.

Now the goat will say good night.

Now the mouse will say good night.

# Now the turkey will say good night.

Now the chick will say good night.

Now the rooster will say good mornin

F  J

# LEARNING PAGE

**SIGHT WORDS:** now, the, will, say

Point to each sight word and read it aloud.

| now | will | say | the |
|-----|------|-----|-----|
| the | say | will | now |
| will | now | say | the |

## BRAIN-BOOSTING QUESTIONS

1. Can you remember all the ways the farm animals say good night? Give it a try.
2. What do you think happens on the farm when the rooster says, "Cock-a-doodle-do"?

## EXTRA

What sounds do other animals make—on the farm, around your neighborhood, or in the wild? Make a list, adding to it every time you think of a new animal's individual sound.

# Welcome to the world of Todd Parr!

Todd inspires and empowers children around the world with fun, positive messages.

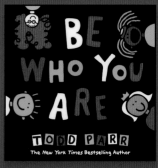

Stories by Todd Parr and Liza Charlesworth
Cover art © 2022 by Todd Parr
Cover design by Lynn El-Roeiy
Cover © 2022 Hachette Book Group, Inc.

LITTLE, BROWN & COMPANY
LB kids
NEW YORK    BOSTON

Visit us at LBYR.com
toddparr.com
978-0-316-30249-4
Not for Individual Resale

# FUNNY FOODS

TODD PARR

# FUNNY FOODS

TODD PARR

LITTLE BROWN & COMPANY
LB kids

Monsters like funny foods.
He eats rocks!

# Monsters like funny foods.
## She eats socks!

Monsters like funny foods.
He eats blocks!

Monsters like funny foods.
She eats clocks!

Monsters like funny foods.
He eats plants!

Monsters like funny foods.
She eats pants!

Monsters like funny foods.
He eats shells!

Monsters like funny foods.
She eats bells!

# Monsters like funny foods.

She eats cars!

Monsters like funny foods.
He eats stars!

F ★ G  H ♥ I ★ J

# LEARNING PAGE

**SIGHT WORDS:** like, he, she

Point to each sight word and read it aloud.

| like | she | like | he |
|------|------|------|------|
| he | she | he | like |
| she | like | he | she |

## BRAIN-BOOSTING QUESTIONS

1. If you were a monster, what would you eat? Make a silly list.
2. What are your very favorite foods? Talk about them.

## EXTRA

Cook or bake with your family. Make something silly but super delicious, such as green eggs or a funny face pizza.

K

L

☆

M

 R  Q  P  ★  O  ♡  N

# Welcome to the world of Todd Parr!

## Todd inspires and empowers children around the world with fun, positive messages.

Stories by Todd Parr and Liza Charlesworth
Cover art © 2022 by Todd Parr.
Cover design by Lynn El-Roeiy
Cover © 2022 Hachette Book Group, Inc.

LB kids™
NEW YORK BOSTON

Visit us at LBYR.com
toddparr.com
978-0-316-30259-3
Not for Individual Resale

# OCEAN COUNT

TODD PARR

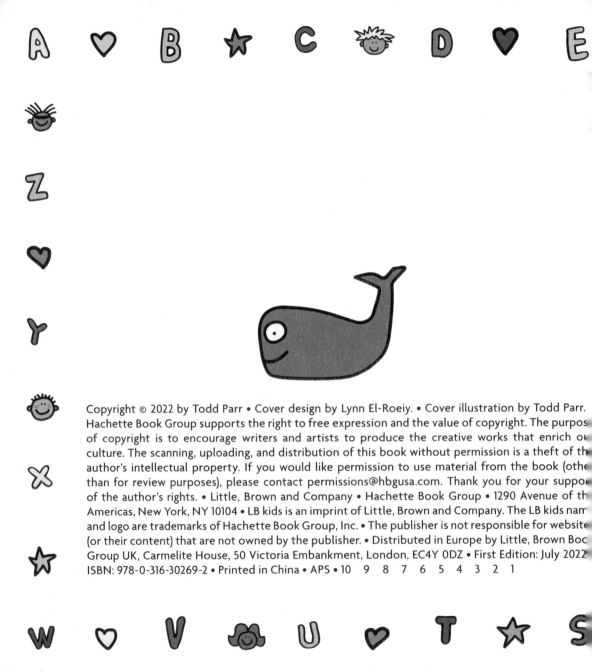

# OCEAN COUNT

## TODD PARR

LITTLE, BROWN & COMPANY

LB kids

# Count one happy fish.

## 1!

# Count two happy crabs.

# 1,2!

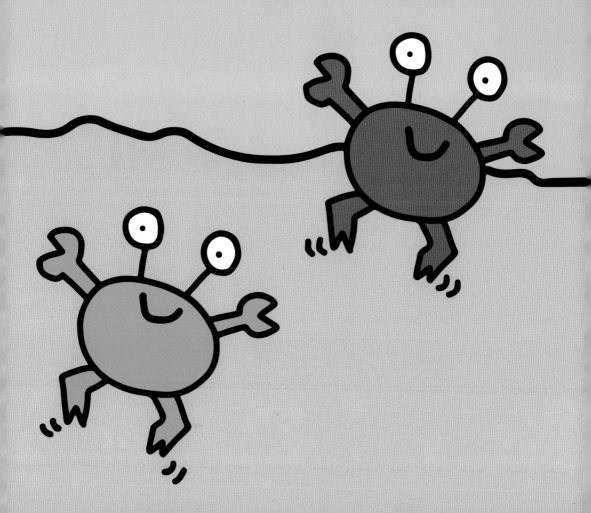

# Count three happy clams.
## 1,2,3!

Count four happy sharks.
1, 2, 3, 4!

# Count six happy eels.

## 1, 2, 3, 4, 5, 6!

Count seven happy dolphins.
1, 2, 3, 4, 5, 6, 7!

# Count eight happy sea stars.
## 1, 2, 3, 4, 5, 6, 7, 8!

# Count nine happy jellyfish.
## 1,2,3,4,5,6,7,8,9!

# Count ten happy whales.
## 1, 2, 3, 4, 5, 6, 7, 8, 9, 10!

G  H ♡ I  J

# LEARNING PAGE

**SIGHT WORDS:** count, one, two, three, four, five, six, seven, eight, nine, ten, happy

Point to each sight word and read it aloud.

| count | three | six | eight |
|-------|-------|-----|-------|
| four | seven | two | ten |
| nine | one | five | happy |

## BRAIN-BOOSTING QUESTIONS

1. Which ocean animal was there the most of? The least of? Which page has a number that matches your own age?
2. Can you think of more animals that live in the ocean? Make a list.

## EXTRA

Read books and explore websites to collect facts about a favorite animal in Ocean Count. Then share what you learned with family and friends.

   P   ♡

# Welcome to the world of Todd Parr!

Todd inspires and empowers children around the world
with fun, positive messages.

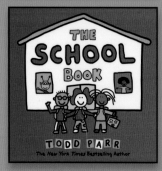

Stories by Todd Parr and Liza Charlesworth
Cover art © 2022 by Todd Parr
Cover design by Lynn El-Roeiy
Cover © 2022 Hachette Book Group, Inc.

LITTLE, BROWN & COMPANY
LB kids™
NEW YORK  BOSTON

Visit us at LBYR.com
toddparr.com
978-0-316-30269-2
Not for Individual Resale